This book belongs to:

....

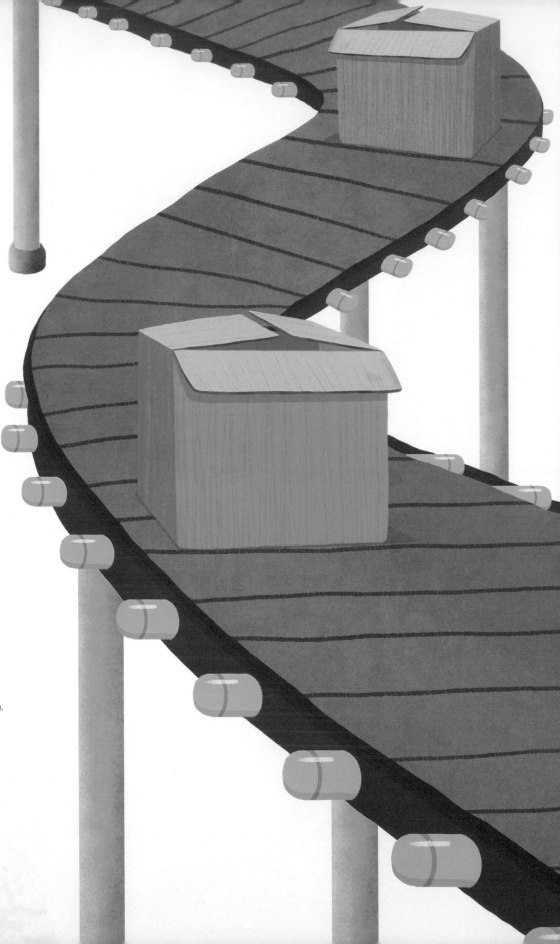

AUTUMN
PUBLISHING

Published in 2022
First published in the UK by Autumn Publishing
An imprint of Igloo Books Ltd
Cottage Farm, NN6 0BJ, UK
Owned by Bonnier Books
Sveavägen 56, Stockholm, Sweden
www.autumnpublishing.co.uk

1122 005
4 6 8 10 9 7 5 3
ISBN 978-1-83903-199-1

Written by Suzanne Fossey
Illustrated by Gisela Bohórquez

Designed by Lee Italiano
Edited by Suzanne Fossey

Printed and manufactured in China

The Life of a Little
CARDBOARD BOX

AUTUMN
PUBLISHING

Folded flat inside a warehouse,
surrounded by my friends,
I waited till a worker
filled me up with odds
and ends.

I was so **excited**. What **adventure** would I find?
"Goodbye," I called out to my friends, as I left my shelf behind.

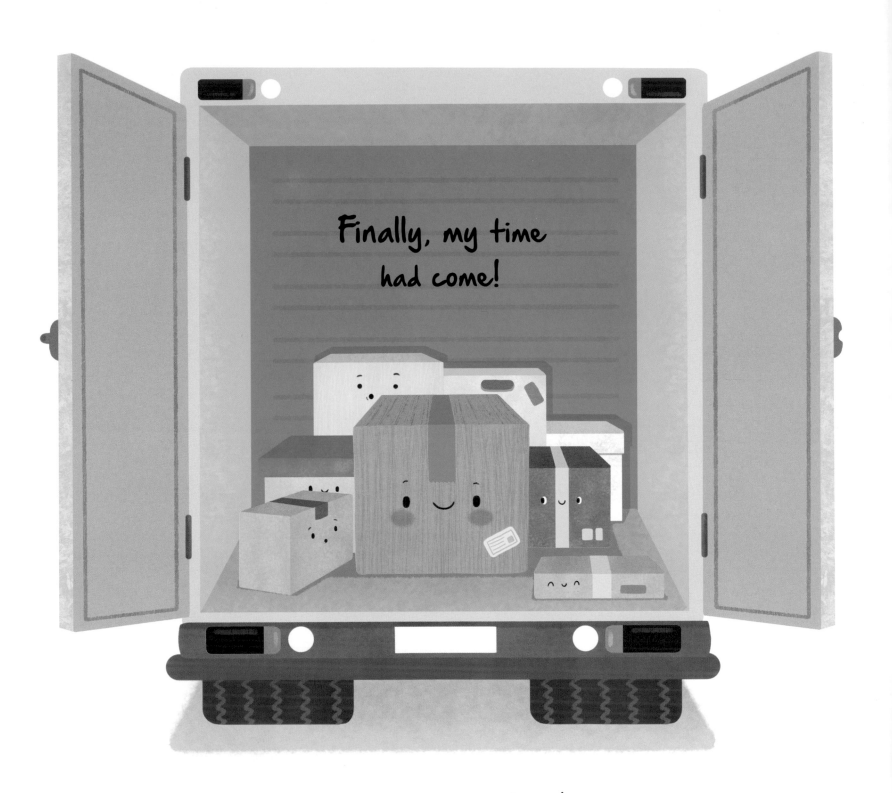

They put me on a truck.

I felt a little nervous:

where would I end up?

I was handed to a little girl, much to her delight.
She **pulled** my tape off, **tipped** me out and **pushed** me out of sight.

A little later
someone **filled** me
with some other
things:

a teddy bear,
a few old books,
a too-small pair
of jeans.

They carried me along the road, then stepped inside a store.

They took the old things out to sell,
then off we went once more.

This time, I joined some other
empty boxes in a car.
We wondered where they'd take us,
and were we going far.

We wound up in a nursery, bright and full of noise. We were going to be **reused** as brand new cardboard toys!

The children
in the nursery
covered me in glue.
They added coloured paper,
and some paper stickers, too.

I was a speedy rocket ship,
they were astronauts in space,
And we had to beat the aliens in an intergalactic race!

Eventually, it had to end.
I began to fall apart.

They put me outside by the bin.
It was getting dark.

A kitten crawled inside me and curled up for the night.

I closed my lid to keep it warm and waited for first light.

When morning came, a truck came by, and off the kitten ran.

I was carried to a **factory**, where

recycling was the plan.

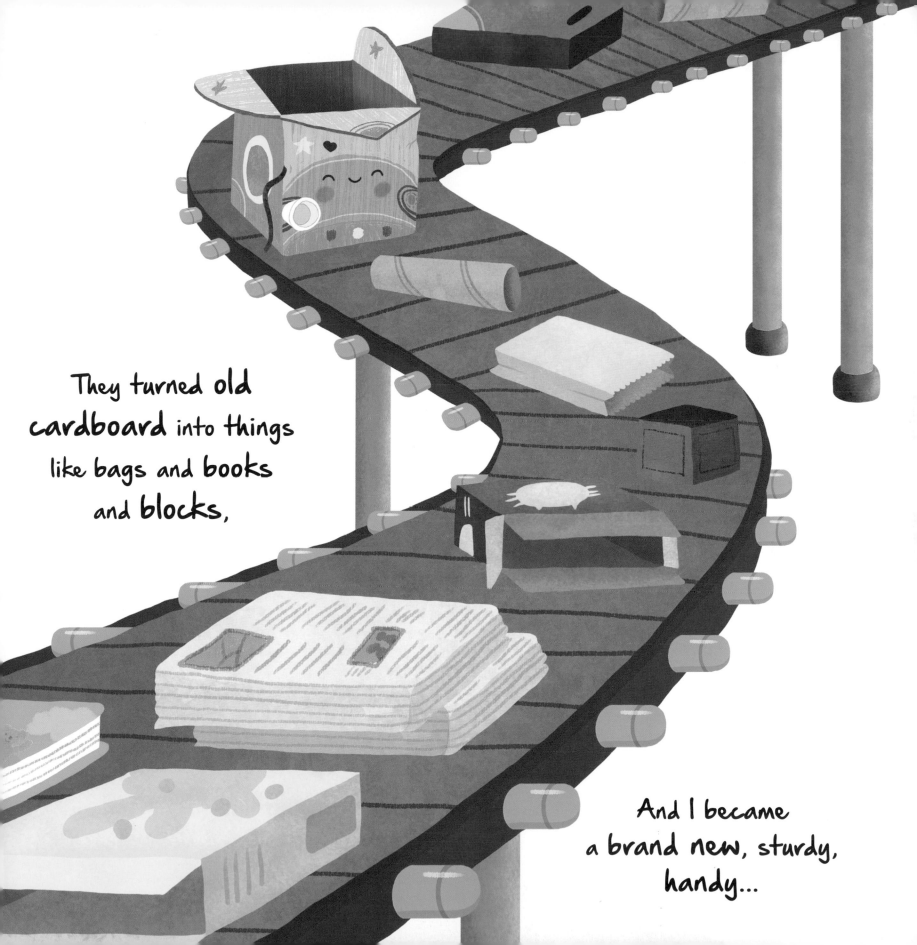

They turned old **cardboard** into things like bags and **books** and **blocks**,

And I became a brand new, sturdy, handy...

... cardboard box!

When you have finished with your cardboard box, there are many ways you can still use it. Why not turn it into a pirate ship, or a finger puppet theatre? You can also put it in a recycling bin. Recycling means that we turn old things into new ones. By recycling cardboard, we can save lots of trees from being cut down. It takes a week for one cardboard box to be recycled, and thousands are recycled at once. They are broken down and made into anything from cereal boxes and greetings cards, to brand new cardboard boxes.